WANTA TRADE WORK FOR RETIREMENT ?

A REALISTIC WAY TO PREPARE FOR RETIREMENT

DOING IT THE WAY YOU WANT

RICHARD A. BEARDSLEY

iUNIVERSE, INC.
NEW YORK   BLOOMINGTON

Wanta Trade Work for Retirement ?
A Realistic Way to Prepare for Retirement

iUniverse books may be ordered through booksellers or by contacting:

iUniverse
1663 Liberty Drive
Bloomington, IN 47403
www.iuniverse.com
1-800-Authors (1-800-288-4677)

Because of the dynamic nature of the Internet, any Web addresses or links contained in this book may have changed since publication and may no longer be valid.

ISBN: 978-1-4401-5936-7 (sc)
ISBN: 978-1-4401-5938-1 (dj)
ISBN: 978-1-4401-5937-4 (ebk)

Printed in the United States of America

Library of Congress Control Number: 2009932272

iUniverse rev. date: 8/26/2009

Dedicated To:

In Honor of Herbert and June Beardsley

In Memory of Jack and Peg Gerrity

In Memory of Roger and Muriel Wood

In Memory of Ben and Doris Spako

In Memory of James D. Spako

CONTENTS

ACKNOWLEDGMENTS

Before we get started, I need to acknowledge this "masterpiece" to many people in my life and work career. Being an unknown writer, I am grateful to IUniverse for granting me the opportunity to express my thoughts on retirement. Cathy Raymond was very patient and very encouraging as I approached various time lines for publication. Ultimately, we got it done.

Let us proceed.

To my wife Kathy Beardsley, I am grateful for your support of my goals and ambitions as I retired and as you continued to work full-time. You worked hard to correlate retirement information and have it in a format for easy reading and for the decision making process. I appreciate all that work!

To my parents Herb and June Beardsley when I look back over the sixty-six years of my life so far, you let my sister Sandy Eckfeldt and me develop and spread our wings while sustaining and supporting us in our challenging times in life. My father was fortunate to retire at sixty years young. He and Mom traveled. However, as they approached their mid-seventies, they had to reduce their travel. I remember taking the Route 66 in 1961 from Chicago to LA. What an experience when I think back on that trip. My wife and I are going to do it again.

To my sister Sandy and brother-in-law Fred Eckfeldt, I want to thank you for hosting the great family gatherings at your house, and for your support of Dad and Mom. Sandy and Fred are dedicated Philadelphia Eagles, Philadelphia Phillies, and Philadelphia Flyers' fans.

To our oldest son Jimi Spako, to his friend Andrea, and to our granddaughter Emily Spako, Mom and I are proud of your progress as you moved to another part of the country to work together to develop a safe and comfortable life style. Jimi has been successful in his employment pursuits even during these times of our economy recession. It is nice to see them a couple times a year. Jimi is a Miami Dolphins' and Philadelphia pro-sports' fan.

To our oldest granddaughter Jessica Hunter, we look forward to your future success when completed your studies in nursing at Neumann College. She lived with us for awhile and was a great motivator to the elder folks who live in our condo complex. She is going to be a superb nurse. Jessica is a dedicated Philadelphia Eagles' and Flyers' fan.

To our youngest daughter Stephanie Beardsley, I appreciate the "light reading" that you provided on retirement. You have been very successful as a Store Manager for American Eagle Outfitters in New Jersey. We cannot leave out your friend Eric Axelson who recently graduated from Rutgers University majoring in accounting and business administration. He also has a job with the U.S. Government. Steph is a Philadelphia Eagle and Phillies' fan. However, Eric and his parents are fully supportive of the Pittsburgh professional teams.

To our son Tim Beardsley, to our daughter-in-law Pat Beardsley, and to their boys Kevin and Nathan Benjamin, I admire your flexibility and enthusiasm as you turned a new leaf in life. Tim and Pat are sharing in the expansion of both their self-employed businesses. It is not easy, but it has been successful. Kevin took a risk in changing jobs and is successfully working with Tim and his Tri-State Lawn Care business. Nathan courageously transferred high schools and now plays football for his new school. Where did I go wrong? This family is dedicated to the Baltimore Ravens.

To John and Mildred McKenny (Pat's parents), I appreciate your patience as I try to learn *American Sign Language*. It is a joy to be in their company. We enjoy being with them on cruises, working at yard sales, and sharing the good times at family gatherings. Until I learn some sign language, we communicate with pen and paper. They are fans of the Baltimore Ravens. John and Mildred: I hope to learn some American Sign Language. However, it is a real challenge for me.

Thanks to our daughter Ann Marie Gillespie and son-in-law Frank Gillespie and our grandchildren Fran, TJ, and Elizabeth for the happy times. We have attended many activities in which Fran, TJ, and Elizabeth participate. Ann Marie has studied hard to become a Registered Emergency Medical Technician, and Frank continues as a successful law officer. WOW, they are constantly on a roll with their children's activities, and "we" could never keep up with them. All are Philadelphia Eagles' fans except for the one grandson Fran who is a fan of the New England Patriots.

To our son Greg Beardsley who lives in Indianapolis with his mother (my ex-wife Susan Wood), I am glad you are doing well enjoying bowling, swimming, and working in the yard. It is great for him to visit us in the summer. Greg likes to swim and works diligently around their house. Needless to say, Greg is an Indianapolis Colts' fan.

Many thanks are extended to Kevin, Lee Ann Reigel, and their children Bailey and Logan for being supportive of their Papa (Herb Beardsley) and "B" (June Beardsley) and for the Christmas Eve Family gatherings. The entire family is Philadelphia Eagles, Phillies, and Flyers' fans.

Devote Enough Time and Effort To Be With Your Family

PREFACE

Why Am I Writing This Book?

There are a number of reasons for this book. I started writing a book in the 1980's. I was going to call it "Men Working with Women—Oh My!" At that time, I was a manager of twenty-five women. That experience, I thought, would be a great topic for a book.

I never got very far because of my family life, dedication to my children, and having a very responsible job. Back in the old days, gas was $.25 per gallon and computers had not taken a full impact in our daily lives. I wrote in long hand my thoughts and an outline as to what I wanted to put on paper. However, after awhile, I decided to let it sit. Over the years, the handwritten papers started to mature at an old age. They became yellow and started to crumble. So, that stopped that project.

As the years continued to move on, the word "retirement" was hitting me smack in the face. That was not a word that we used in our earlier generations. That word was far from our vocabulary. It soon became a household word as we moved into our mid-50's. This book is on the conceptual overview of retirement that was an idea of mine for the last year. As I embarked on retirement, I realized that an educational document was required for us "baby boomers."

I worked in the health industry for over thirty-seven years in the field of patient financial services. Working at Christiana Care Health Services in Delaware, I became very educated and knowledgeable on the workings of Medicare and other HMO insurance. Parts of the job were giving advice to the public on the decisions for selection of a health insurance after retiring. The academic background with Degrees in Accounting and Business Administration has extended me the expertise to approach retirement with the proper knowledge for the future.

Please just remember as you move toward retirement, it does not matter how fast you are going as long as you are going in the right direction. Keep focused on your goals. That will be what you will read and note during the reading of this text. This book provides you with some conceptual ideas and thoughts but not all the answers for retirement. As you read, please think of your detailed thoughts. You will be pleasantly surprised.

Bruce Lee is quoted "If you love life, do not waste time. For time, it is made of life."

You Can Do the Same Thing – Write A Book

INTRODUCTION

I am just a down home guy who was successful as I could be. I am a typical average middle-income fellow, who like many others, have had many interesting challenges in life. Some of the challenges were not pleasant, but what would life be like without a challenge to sharpen your mind and to assist us to understand that life can be better. At times, that negative turned out to be positive.

I worked at the same health care facility as an accountant for over thirty-seven years. I would have liked to move on at times. However, when I got my thoughts in line with my mind, I knew that I had to make this employer my career. I realized that my contributions would be successful. Again, there were many challenges. However, I survived those occupational challenges and became a better person.

I am inspired to write this text for the education of "baby boomers" who want to retire. Preparing for retirement can be a stressful time in your life, especially with the state of the world economy (2009). This book will give you the information to proceed toward your retirement day with pleasure and excitement.

In an article from the June 16, 2008, (Wilmington, Delaware) *The News Journal*, it was reported that Americans are living longer and living better lives. For many years, it has been a known fact that women tend to live longer. The extended longevity is contributed to maintaining a good exercise program and eating healthier. That means giving up smoking, not drinking to excess, and walking to stay in good health. Another point made in the article is where you live. Learn about cancer clusters in your area, and learn about the local environment.

According to that June sixth article, life expectancy has increase as noted below:

	2008	**2005**
Women	80.7	79.1
Men	75.4	74.3
Average	78.1	77.8

Let us cut through all these and now move on to the text of this book.

Face Retirement with A Challenge Or Two

ONE

Even the Thought of Retirement... Why?

It all began in the fall of 2007........

My wife Kathy is three and half years younger than I am. Almost by surprise, we realized that it was time for us to seriously think about the word **retirement** after some challenging changes at my place of employment. Let me first say, I am not bashing my previous employer. As I accumulated more years and with the change of management, I was left-out of meetings that affected my duties, was one of the last in line to get computer upgrades, and was ignored when offering suggestions to improve the job productivity. I no longer had the opportunity to use my talents to train employees and present documentation and policies that would have contributed to the improvement of information gathering. What happened to me happens to many older workers. I was able to survive it and prepared for the future on the avenue that my wife and I decided.

Call retirement anything you want. It is the new horizon; it is a new lease on life; it is a new sunrise. Whatever you call it, it is your need to prepare for your new career. Use retirement to be your time for personal growth, developing interests outside of work, and establishing high self-esteem that will lessen stress.

1

Kathy and I started to compile information on retirement. I really planned to work into my late sixties. However, who wants to miss out on the finer things of life?

Retirement

According to *The New Webster's Dictionary"* (1993), retirement is defined as the following:

"Retiring is giving up an active participation in a business or in an occupation."

To me, retirement is like hitting a big jackpot in Atlantic City or in Vegas. Retirement should put a smile on your face. Retirement is when you are ready, and I was ready. When you decide to retire, do it. Thank goodness for retirement because it is going to be more rewarding than work. Think of retirement as being a savings account. Then watch it build interest. Thank God for good health.

Okay, it was time to think clearly and be thankful for our good health and our desire to travel that "Old Route 66." Kathy and I started to dig into the reality of retirement. We did the following:

Studied the benefits of health care

Researched Medicare and Medi-Gap

Studied in detail our financial outlook

Considered what we would do after retiring – beyond relaxing and sleeping. We did not want to sleep our lives away

Started researching the web on aging and healthy activities

Started to pay more attention to related articles in the printed media

Visited the Social Security Administration

Talked to our human resources departments

Discussed options with our company's financial advisors

Attended workshops on retirement

I initially planned to retire on June 5, 2009, at the ripe old age of sixty-six. At that age, I would receive full Social Security benefits. That seemed so far off and seemed that I would be too old to do anything. Retiring too late means that when you retire, you have no other ideas and no goals to accomplish. Suggestion: Write yourself a letter on retirement. Then, share it with the family after you are fully retired. You will find it interesting and motivational. Take my word, it is fun.

After some serious research, after some serious meetings, after some serious scanning of spread sheets, Kathy and I agreed that I could retire in January of 2009, at sixty-five-and-a-half years old and take about a $350 cut in my Social Security benefits, which is not prorated between the ages of sixty-five and sixty-six.

When reading the daily paper, I usually glance at the obituaries. I am so surprised to read of many people under the age of fifty-five. That is another good reason to think about retirement at a young age.

"Do Things While You Are Young"
(Herbert and June Beardsley, Parents)

For a Christmas (2007) gift, our youngest daughter Stephanie gave us a book to read about the preparation for retirement. It was very inspiring and set my mind at ease. I knew that our decision for me to cut loose from work in January of 2009 was absolutely the right and just thing to do, not only for me but for my employer. Whatever the United States and world economies were at the time, it was time for me to go. When I look back, maybe I should have retired a year or so earlier. Oh, well, we cannot look back but have to move forward.

Another thought: Remember when the grandchildren spent a weekend with you, then they went home. Subsequently, their parents had to deprogram them. Well, that is the same with retirement. You need to reprogram from the work environment to retirement. Make retirement fun, not a job. Think what excited you in the past and has lingered in your mind for all those years. Then, start it again. Be challenged. Look at it as the beginning. Think of it as a new day today.

Think of yourself as a flower being planted in the ground. It is dormant while you are working but full of life when you retire. Plant the seed and watch it grow. Research your options as compared to your retirement goals. Evaluate your options, start on a plan with those options, keep your dream open, and do it!

In the pages that follow, I have reduced the reading to the basic need with partial empty pages for you to make your own notes and jot down your own ideas. I have tried not to be redundant and not make this "heavy" reading. This is written by an U. S. citizen who has been through the workings of Medicare, Medicaid, and all the other challenges preparing for retirement.

So, let us begin and enjoy the good times of life and make life better in our later years. Be grateful for what you have!

4

"Let's Roll"
Lisa Beamer, *Wife of 9/11 Hero Todd Beamer*

What Does the Word "Retirement" Mean to You?

_____

_____

_____

What Are Your Pros and Cons on Retirement?

PROS   CONS

_____   _____

_____   _____

_____   _____

_____   _____

Personal Notes:

*You Can Be Just As Productive At Retirement As You Were At Work
You Can Feel Self-Motivated With Retirement As At Work
You Can Accomplish Good Things during Retirement Just
Like You Did At Work*

TWO

When to Discuss Retirement with Management

I cannot suggest a good time to meet with your managers to enlighten them on your plans to retire. In the 1940's up until the 1960's, some employers let an employee depart as soon as the notice was given.

Before making that final decision to retire, ask yourself some of these questions:

Yes or No

Are you happy with work? _____

If not, will retirement make you happy? _____

Can you think of things that make you happy? _____

Can you set your goals and challenges for retirement life?_____

Can you contribute your talents and interests to the community during retirement? _____

Can your employer survive without you? _____

(Just being light hearted with that question.)

Why? The philosophy during those days was that once an employee had decided to depart, they would be totally unproductive. Well, the law has changed and that cannot be done now-a-days. It depends on the position you hold. Do what you think is right. I will admit that once Kathy and I agreed on decision that I would leave January 9, 2009, my attitude, behavior, and just overall life changed for the best. I can remember when receiving my "military orders" to rotate back to The States from Vietnam. Remember Jackie Gleason saying: *"Oh, How Sweet It Is."* With retirement, I knew the end was near. I felt so good even though I had twelve months to go before announcing my intentions to my management staff on November 4, 2008.

PS Note: I wrote the contents of this part of the chapter below about seven months before retirement on January 9, 2009, or about five months before I initially was going to give my notice on Election Day November 4, 2008.

Please read on to see my final decision for presenting my notice to management. In my organization, a two-week notice for departure was the policy. So, I worked back from the date of January 9, 2009.

A two-week notice would be Friday, December 26, 2008.

Now was that enough time?

_____*Yes*   _____*No*

How about on Wednesday, December 24, 2008, of which would be my Christmas gift to them?

_____*Yes*   _____*No*

Over a period of time, I mellowed a little more and as a courtesy to give my notice on Tuesday, December 2, 2008. I further melt down and had to think deep:

8

How long have you have been with your employer?

_____

How did they treat you over the long run?

_____

What impact did you have on your company over the years?

_____

Overall were you treated fairly?

_____

What are some of your thoughts of your employer?

_____

Please think deep and hard of the positives of your job.

_____

This is the second "retirement game plan" that Kathy and I developed in December of 2007:

Retirement is here!   **Friday**   **January 9, 2009**

Schedule meeting with   **Monday**   **November 3, 2008**
management

Meet with managers   **Tuesday**   **November 4, 2008**
(What a coincidence, it was Election Day)

To me, this was a very fair and courtesy time frame.

> *PS Note II:* The above was written about eight months before discussing my intentions to retire with management.

Below was my final decision of my notice to management:

I guess that I felt a sense of loyalty for my company. I wanted to be more than fair to my employer because of the professional positions that I held. I decided to give management more time to decide the status of my position.

Retirement date	**Friday**	**January 9, 2009**
Scheduled meeting with management	**Thursday**	**October 2, 2008**
Met with management	**Tuesday**	**October 7, 2008**

Do you think that is a very fair schedule for management to make their decision on the replacement and/or reorganizing? I felt good about that.

Now, It Is Time for You to Brainstorm Your Schedule

_____

_____

_____

_____

_____

_____

Make Your Own Comfort Level

THREE

It Is Okay To Make It Official

Once Kathy and I made the decision that it was okay for me to retire, I quietly started to prepare for my departure:

Updated my job descriptions along with the policies and procedures

Prepared a list of topics for the transition

Started to discard old papers and not keep papers that were also stored electronically

Updated my files for the person to succeed me

Prepared my agenda for the meeting when giving my notice

Prepared an officially typed document that would be e-mailed to management as confirmation of our meeting

Drafted an e-mail to send to my family, my co-workers, friends, and subcontractors at the appropriate time after the meeting

As I approached that management meeting, I have to admit that I occasionally found that my concentration on the job was drifting. However, it did not take long to refocus my mind on the work at hand. Why did my concentration linger? I cannot answer that. Maybe it was the fear of the unexpected or the excitement of retirement.

When making your verbal announcement to management of your plans to retire, I strongly suggest that you keep it positive. You will be thought more highly as a happy employee not just another disgruntled employee. In that meeting with management, I planned to discuss the following:

Be specific on the exact date and time of retirement

Explain that this was an easy decision but a challenging one at the same

Explain that I have done all I can for my employer, and that there is nothing else that I can do to contribute at this point of your career

It is time to move on to the greater things of life

Explain that I have my "ducks in line" as noted below:

1. Medicare is set up

2. Employer health plan has been reviewed in detail

3. Social Security benefits start in February

4. Retirement investments have been reviewed

5. Employer pension is set up

6. Retirement plan structured

7. I am going to write this book

8. I am going to get involved with trying to make local political changes

Let them know that you are fine and ready for the "Retirement Day." Present them an agenda for a transition plan. For me, I planned to request not to have any farewell dinner or party. Communicate your decision to the staff. I would suggest to management during the meeting that you will take care of announcing your retirement to your coworkers as soon as the meeting is adjourned. It can be a short e-mail explaining your plans.

Plan to make it your meeting not theirs. Plan to depart the meeting shaking hands and thanking them for their time. The most important item is for you to be strong, be diplomatic, and be in control of situation. The ball will be in their of the court, and you have nothing to fear except a good time.

YES, You Have To Control Your Own Life Style

FOUR

You Really Want to Know What Happened

Okay, here is the real story of my meeting with management when I alerted them on my plans "to get out of here!"

I scheduled the appointment three days in advance explaining in my e-mail that I needed to meet at 9:00 a.m. on Tuesday, October 7, 2008, to discuss my future with the company. I will insert now how I felt leading up to that meeting. I must admit as I approached closer to the meeting I felt some anxiety and at times felt a little down. Maybe it was the fear of the unknown. However, after a good night's rest, I was back on track and ready to face "The Mother of All Meetings."

I brought to the meeting the following:

1. An official typed letter detailing my retirement plans.

2. An agenda of my suggested transition plan.

3. A transition plan including a detailed list of the job responsibilities.

4. I placed in my brief case a "Count Down to Retirement Clock" given to me by my sister.

5. I also stuffed an "over the hill" hat in the brief case which was given to me by my grandchildren on my sixth birthday.

I started the meeting by stating that I have a few things to say and to please give me a chance to express my agenda.

1. I was very positive about my thirty-seven plus years at the organization.

2. I stated that I have accomplished much with the organization.

3. That I have done all I can at this point of my career.

4. There is not much more that I can contribute.

5. I alerted them that I am retiring effective January 9, 2009, at 3:30 p.m.

At that point, I pulled out my count-down clock and placed it on the desk which showed ninety-one actual days until January 9, 2009. I also pulled out my "over-the-hill" hat and put it on. This stirred a lot of laughs and lightened up the meeting. I presented my suggestions for transition. I assured management that my policies and procedures were up-to-date, that Kathy and I are very excited about moving to a new career and new adventures. I reiterated that I was ready for retirement and felt very comfortable. The last point that I wanted to make was that I wanted to depart quietly and with little fanfare. However, they encouraged me to have a farewell gathering. I agreed.

The one item that I wanted to cover was notification of my coworkers. I explained my game plan to e-mail my management to confirm this meeting. I would e-mail the staff on my decision to retire. However, at the suggestion of my manager, it was decided that he would make the announcement directly to the staff after the meeting. It was an excellent suggestion. The staff was totally surprised and appreciated being notified before the other departments.

My approach worked very positively for this meeting. It was positive and was upbeat. It was informational so that management could take the three months to develop a reorganization plan. We left shaking hands and all were smiling, especially me.

Now, let the transition begin and let the fun begin as well. All that pre-existing anxiety is now down the drain. Let the real fun start.

That is the real story behind announcing my decision for the future.

What Would Be Your Game Plan?
What Would You Do Differently?

_____

_____

_____

_____

_____

_____

Yes, I Can Achieve Something in My Retirement Career That Will Make Me Proud

FIVE

It Will Be the Best Time of Your Golden Years

"Retirement" is not an ugly word. Rather it is a good word. It is a word that should make us feel good. As I write this part of the book, I have about "318 actual days" left until January 9, 2009. I am really excited about the thought of retirement. I am not saying that I would have everything worked out to the minute, but I have a great concept of retirement and what it is all about. Some people enjoy working until they die. That is not me. Here are some reasons for "doing it your way":

Do a self-evaluation thinking of good and challenging things

Write yourself a letter, and then read it six months after full retirement

Call your own schedule

Be the "Master of Leisure"

Do something for a purpose, make it fun

Be cool!

Do not have to report to a boss

Report to yourself

You do not have to accept projects from the boss

Word of Caution: Your spouse might delegate some duties

Call your own shots

Set your own agenda

Share your talents with others surrounding you

Be flexible

Be spontaneous

Spend time with your family

Take up a hobby or two

Do a self-evaluation for a second time

Focus on what you are doing right. Please do not dwell on the negative. Do not make retirement an empty space. Be confident and be ambitious in this transition of life.

What are Your Interests?   **How Would You Get Started?**

_____   _____

_____   _____

_____   _____

_____   _____

I enjoy photography and organizing albums for the future generations. That might sound odd because it does clutter our condo. It is a hobby of mine that keeps me active and involved at special occasions. Help your spouse with things that she is doing while still working, such as taking the grandchildren to school or helping your sons with their businesses.

Calls for flexibility but also calls for some routine

Get involved with your Church

Educate yourself taking *American Sign Language*

Do things that you have not thought of doing

I am writing this book for my satisfaction even if it does not get on the shelves. (This is a later comment: Writing this book gave me plenty of insight into what is retirement. I have had fun doing it even if it does not make the *New York Times* best seller list).

Make a List of Books That You Would Write

_____

_____

_____

_____

Start writing a book. You will find that your built-in abilities will flow and the fun has just begun. On the other

hand, let me warn you not to get discouraged. There will be good days and some challenging days when the words just do not flow as you would like.

I am helping more with the "condo chores and projects." There is time to do the laundry. Time can be found to do the weekly cleaning so when Kathy arrives home there is little for her to do.

Kathy and I are primary caregivers to my parents as they age toward their nineties. I did not expect this responsibility on my retirement day. You can get the ball rolling to make a difference for senior citizens because I am one now. I want to work with the local politicians to change the law so that seniors over sixty-five years that their loan and credit claims do not appear on their credit reports. Make a difference and feel good doing it. We, the people, need to take care of the elderly.

Challenge yourself. You need to be self-motivated. Low self-esteem will lead to depression and leave you with no motivation to move on or to do anything. With retirement, you grow faithfully and mentally. So, enjoy the later years. Do not "wish" but do it. Follow through with your wishes and dreams.

"Plan It and You Can Do It"
(Richard A. Beardsley, Retired)

How about considering some of these ideas and then list your ideas at the end of this chapter:

Go to your local high school's outdoor games during the week.

Attend local little league games.

Attend your local college games. There are plenty in our area at the University of Delaware, Delaware State University, and Wesley College.

Attend a minor league weekday afternoon game. We have learned that these minor league games are just as exciting as the majors and the cost is significantly less. A half hour north of us is the Wilmington (Delaware) Blue Rocks and a half hour south of us is the Aberdeen (Maryland) Iron Birds.

Take $10 and go to the local racetrack. Enjoy the races and not bet too much. Know your limit.

Take $25 to the local casino and know when to stop.

Leisure time is doing something that is useful for your community, for your Church, *Habitat for Humanity* (www. habitat.org) and for your family.

Attend free seminars at the local YMCA, at the Senior Center, at your local college, and those sponsored by your city or community.

Volunteer at the local Blood Bank, hospital, or Senior Center.

Be a speaker at a community function to share your life experience. This is one hidden talent that my new management group did not observe.

Attend your grandchildren's school activities and even volunteer. Be a mentor at your grandchildren's schools. You will have a lot to offer from your experience in life.

Travel to visit where you were born and see the how things have changed. Recently, Kathy and I traveled to Niagara Falls, New York, where I was born. Oh, how things have changed in certain areas. Then, we crossed the bridge to Grand Island, New York, where our family lived for four years. Interesting enough the old home has not changed too much. Some of the areas are still wide open. That was over fifty-five years ago when Dad was transferred to Wilmington, Delaware.

There are many historical sites around the United States. Be a tour guide at one of your local historical areas. You see seniors presenting tours in Key West, Florida, Gettysburg, Pennsylvania, and Williamsburg, Virginia, for example. You will not only have fun, you will learn about the history and how this country was developed.

Meet your spouse for lunch. (Kathy added "This is a great idea").

I can go on and on, but you need to be creative.

Do not be a creature of habit. You do not have to do the same thing every day. You do not have to eat the same thing every day. You do not have to be on a time schedule and account for every minute. If you get in a rut, change your course of action or change the ways you do things. Do not get discouraged.

Jot It Down Before You Forget

_____

_____

_____

Yes, I Can Commit Time to Indulge In Creative Goals

SIX

Think Positive and Be Healthy

"Attitude Not Age Determines Energy" (Robert Schuller)

I will be the first to admit when I started in the civilian work force in 1971 the word retirement was not in my English language. Life moves so quickly. We all must slow down and think toward the future.

Learn the difference between an annuity and mutual funds. There is a difference that could result in lost investments if the wrong plan is selected. I suggest that you consult a financial advisor. It will be worth it. Get enrolled in a mutual fund program at your place of employment or at your bank. This is not only a tax shelter program but a quiet way to build toward your retirement. Social Security and your pension (if there is any) will not support you and your spouse during the later years.

Stay in good health. Here are some basic thoughts to consider:

1. Do not miss your doctor appointments.

2. Do not be shy asking your kids or grandchildren to transport you to appointments.

3. Take your medication to all your doctor appointments.

4. Take your medicine at the prescribed times.

5. Be a good person and follow your physician's instructions.

6. Get your blood pressure, sugar, and cholesterol checked routinely. Free test units are available at the drug stores, super markets, and fitness centers.

7. Do not smoke because it is a killer and increases the aging process.

8. Stay away from second hand smoke.

9. Do not drink alcohol to excess.

10. Watch your diet and weight. This is one of the hardest goals to maintain in the aging process. We all work really hard on our weight control as we get older. Yes, it maybe discouraging. You need to focus, set a personal goal and just do it. Eat plenty of fresh fruits and vegetables.

11. Always slap on plenty of sunscreen, hat, sunglasses, and reduce your time in sun.

12. Stay away from prescription drugs if at all possible. I should talk. I had to take medicine for hypertension, anxiety, cholesterol, and depression while I was working full time. As I approached the R-Day (Retirement Day), I discussed with my doctor what medications I could gradually eliminate.

13. For me, the results are that I will start weaning off two prescriptions. One was for anxiety for better night's rest and

the other was for depression. That was a monthly savings of $30.00. Not bad little change to be thrown in my bank jar.

14. I recently learned that my eighty-nine year old parents only take two medications daily. That is unbelievable at their age. That shows good living can keep you on top at the game while growing older.

15. One other suggestion that I can offer is ask your primary care physician for free samples that can save you a few dollars.

List Your Medications

_____

_____

_____

_____

_____

16. Ask your doctor these questions:

Is there any problem of which you should be aware?

What do you need to do to overcome this challenge?

What are the implications?

Are these medications okay to take?

17. Definitely stay away from over-the-counter diet pills. I never tried them because they are too scary. There are too

many negative results as far as I am concerned. My primary care physician totally agrees.

Exercise to your heart's content. Do that physical activity for at least thirty minutes daily. I am not a muscle bound guy. I never made the high school football team; never made the basketball team; never got by the first cut for the baseball team. In fact, I could not even make the track team. However, that did not stop me from playing football in the back field; did not stop me from playing basketball in our garage that my parents (Herb and June) set up; did not stop me from playing baseball in the back field; and did not stop me from enlisting in the Unites States Air Force. I served our country for four years of which one year was a tour of duty in Vietnam during 1966.

Now, let me return to the real life. The aging process makes it the way you want to make it. In a nut shell, you must be self-motivated, must be active, and take care of your body. Here are a few ideas that I have implemented:

1. Walk until you cannot walk anymore but *Walk Do Not Run*

2. Go to The Mall and walk in the mornings (leave your credit card at home)

3. Go to the park and enjoy the outdoors

4. Start off with fifty situps and soon you will be doing one hundred

5. Swim to your heart's content. According to my primary care physician swimming is the best exercise

6. Use the stairs as much as possible even on your vacation

7. Control your blood pressure by getting it checked monthly. There are many places that offer blood pressure checks. Take

advantage of the free testing at your local pharmacy (drug store), periodically at church, and at the Senior Center

8. Purchase your own blood pressure instrument to take your own "BP"

9. Stay calm and low key to assist to control stress. Yes, stress can affect you even while retired

10. Do something to help relax

11. Detect diabetes early, purchase your own "acc-u-check" instrument. Use it daily or as directed by your doctor

12. If life and activities get boring, step back and look at yourself

13. Ask yourself how to get out of that rut

14. Write yourself another letter

15. A smile says it all

16. A smile leads to a positive attitude, and you will feel better

Now, It Is Your Turn

What Can You Add To Stay Health?	*What Can You Add To the Exercise List?*
_____	_____
_____	_____
_____	_____
_____	_____

_____ _____

_____ _____

_____ _____

Yes, You Can Make Yourself Feel Better

Stay Healthy –Eat Fresh Fruits And Vegetables

SEVEN

Money is Meant to be Spent But on Yourselves

The financial aspect of retirement is an important component of retirement. It is important to prepare for a long retirement. Take into consideration how inflation and/or a recession can affect your retirement. Yes, I know that money is needed to live a comfortable life until "our ticket is punched to go to The Lord." This is a statement that my late father-in-law Roger Wood used before his trip to the Lord on August 12, 2008. You do not want to run out of money when you need it the most. Enjoy life while you are young and bubbly, while you are in good health, and while you have the finances to do it. My parents (Herb and June) have reemphasized many times "to do things while you are young."

There are a number of ways to financially prepare for retirement. First, start your financial planning in your twenties. May I suggest that you give a copy of this book to your children and other members of your family. Again, I am being somewhat redundant. However, I must correlate the subjects in order to bring unity to the subject of each chapter.

Use your employer tax shelter mutual fund program

Invest in certificates of deposit (CD's)

Note: Be careful of independent agents as shown on *NBC Dateline* segment in 2007 who could attempt to scam you

Check with your Better Business Bureau

Have payroll deductions directly to your savings account

Have payroll deductions for U.S. Savings Bonds

Stay with your employer as long as possible to build up your tenure and your "vested pension"

Consult a financial advisor to invest money in the Stock Market

I know plenty of elderly folks think that they have to save their money for the family when they die. My sister added that she attended a financial advisor seminar in which the speaker said "that you did proper financial planning when the check bounces for your funeral."

We earned that money. We darn well deserve to keep it and use it. Yes, it is okay to set money aside for the trip of your dreams, funerals, assisted living, and nursing care. Those are just a few things that come to mind right now. In preparation for the financial portion of retirement, a budget needs to be developed like any other budget while you were working. There are many advantages to mutual funds and drawing from it monthly like a pay check. You need to consult with your personal financial advisor or your human resources financial advisor to develop a game plan and a back up plan.

To reduce costs as they rise, apply for senior discounts for school taxes, property taxes, utility bills, and health care.

What Is More Important – Money, Your Health, or Your Ambitions?

When developing a retirement budget, you need to think about how to invest your retirement pay, vacation pay, mutual fund, U.S. Savings Bonds, Social Security, and other investments. With the U.S. economy floundering (since 2008 into 2009), extra precautions have to be considered. Here is what Kathy and I did:

1. I retired during the first week of the year (January 9, 2009).

2. We hired a financial advisor to assist Kathy and me to make the right decisions.

3. At the advice of our financial advisor, I rolled over my pension lump sum into a mutual fund.

4. I also received pay for my unused vacation and sick time.

5. We immediately converted that to a certificate of deposit.

6. Months before retirement, we developed a retirement budget knowing that we would have to cut back on some leisure activities.

7. Subsequently, we took into consideration my Social Security payments and decided how much we had to draw each month from our mutual funds.

8. With our mutual funds, we could withdraw a predetermined amount each month as well as a one time per year withdraw a lump sum for that special vacation, wedding, for example.

All that I can suggest is to work hard on your budget and do your homework to live comfortably during your senior years.

Yes, You Can Make the Most of Your Money and Feel Good About It

EIGHT

Oh, Those Government Options
Yes, It Can Be Confusing

Let us sort out the Government Benefits of Social Security and Medicare. It can be a bit confusing. So, what can we do to make it easier? There is no way to make it easier. It takes time to study and ask questions. Review all the options. This is the course of action that Kathy and I pursued, and we were pleased with the results:

Talk to your Human Resources representative on what is involved

Discuss options with your health provider

Use the "Social Security" web pages to access information

www.socialsecurity.gov

Visit your local Social Security Administration to obtain information

This section is Medicare. You will need to study and ask questions. This information can be obtained from your local Social Security Administration:

www.medicare.gov
1-800-633-4227

- **Medicare Part A** is hospital insurance. This pays for some of costs for inpatient hospitalization and certain followup care. For example, it includes skilled nursing care and home health care. For the most part, this benefit involves no premiums if you have worked and contributed through the Medicare withholding system. There is no specific guideline to cover each individual. I suggest that you contact your local Social Security Office for more details.

- **Medicare Part B** is medical insurance. It primarily pays for doctor visits, some outpatient hospital services, radiology services, lab tests, certain type of medical equipment—such as wheelchairs. There is a premium for Medicare Part B. In 2008, the monthly premium was $96.40. For 2009, the premium is $115. Again, please discuss with the staff of your local Social Security Administration.

Note: If you hear the term "Traditional Medicare," it refers to Medicare Part A and B.

- **Medicare Part C** is an HMO health plan. You will need to discuss this with your commercial insurance company. Please keep in mind that the lowest premiums are not always the best plan. Low premiums could result in higher deductibles. Also, your premiums are not guaranteed for life. Ask about pre-existing situations. Be careful of policy changes. Check carefully to assure the policies overlap for short period of time. Do not leave gaps without coverage.

- **Medicare Part D** is the outpatient prescription plan. You will need to discuss in more detail with the Social Security Office.

  Personal Note: What I have recorded above are only suggestions and gives you food for thought. I can only suggest that you ask questions and ask more questions until you feel comfortable to make a decision. Check with your State's Insurance Commissioner and/or research at your State's Website.

If you continue to work past sixty-five years old, you should visit the Social Security office to sign up for Medicare three months prior to your sixty-fifth birthday. I found it much easier to call my local Social Security Office to schedule an appointment. I was taken ten minutes earlier than the appointment while others were still in the waiting room. The entire process took less than twenty minutes. My Medicare Card arrived in the mail about two weeks later. You will need the following to enroll in Medicare:

Original Social Security card

Driver's license

Original birth certificate with a raised seal

Note: The above is what I needed when I enrolled for Medicare in early 2008. With constant changes in tightening the U.S. security policies, please contact your local Social Security Administration office to confirm what is required prior to your visit.

You probably have more questions now than you ever had. That is okay. Kathy and I were so confused at first that we could not see straight. That is the objective of this book. Not only to keep me busy but to assist you to make an easier transition. I also suggest that you start working on your retirement research four or five years from your target date to retire.

What I found interesting after I enrolled in Medicare, I started to receive "junk mail" from insurance companies and pharmacies on the Medicare Prescription Plan D. I did not ask or request that information. However, the advertisements kept arriving. I wonder how they got my name and address.

For the most part, you are not eligible for Medicare until you reach the age of sixty-five. You are eligible for Social Security benefits at sixty-two years old. You should be receiving a Social Security pamphlet each year outlining your benefits. I could not collect full benefits until I was sixty-six years old. Kathy would have to work until sixty-seven years old to receive full benefits.

Annoying, isn't it?

For example, when I retired on January 9, 2009, I was sixty-five and half years old. If I had worked full time at the same company until sixty-six, I would have received full benefits that amounted to about $350 more a month. That was not worth it for me with my company lump sum pension, with my mutual fund, and with Social Security even with this faltering economy.

Here again, you have to sign up for these benefits three months prior to your retirement. When I signed up for the Social Security benefits, I needed the following:

Your Check Off List

Signed form from Human Resources   _____

Original birth certificate with raised seal   _____

Original Social Security card   _____

Driver's license   _____

Latest Federal Tax Return   _____

Latest W-2 _____

Latest pay stub _____

Marriage License(s) _____

If appropriate, divorce papers _____

Passport _____

If in the military, DD-214 _____

Annual Social Security Statements _____

Here is what really occurred when I enrolled for Social Security benefits. In late August of 2008, I called the local Social Security Administration to schedule an appointment. It was scheduled for 2:15 p.m. on Thursday, September 11, 2008, a day not to be forgotten in American History. It was explained to me that I would receive a letter confirming the time and what documents are required.

Two days later I did receive the confirmation letter outlining what documents were required. I arrived at the Social Security Office about thirty minutes before the appointment. I electronically signed in. I was asked to come in their cubicle twenty minutes before the actual scheduled meeting. I was surprised that I was asked to get started with the process that early (better than some doctor offices).

With the proper documents in hand, the entire process lasted about thirty-five minutes. I was so happy coming out of the Social Security office, I was jumping for joy and called KATHY. All I can say if you study, read, and ask questions before your appointment, you will zip through the process without any problem.

Have Medicare Card -- Will Travel

What Questions Come to Mind?

_____

_____

_____

_____

What Is The $64,000-Question?

NINE

Let the Countdown Begin

When I served in Vietnam during 1966-67, GI's had count down calendars attached to their lockers or on the wall. Each day we would cross off a day until we would rotate back to "The Good Ole USA." Here is a tidbit of information: Do you know what the GI's favorite song was and probably still is?

"I Left My Heart in San Francisco" (Tony Bennett).

Once Kathy and I made the decision for me to retire, ironically my sister Sandy and brother-in-law Fred gave us a count down clock. It started with "532 days, 10 hours, 5 minutes and 10 seconds" to June 5, 2009. It is a neat gizmo and neat to see it sitting on our kitchen counter.

So, I did a little creative thinking before receiving that gift. This concept depends on the type of work you do. I worked in an office environment with a computer. The end of each month was called "End of the Month Closing." Okay, here are some little ideas that I used to count down to that "R-Day."

By November of 2007, I decided to retire on January 9, 2009. I started the countdown with the number of "End of the Month

Close Outs." There were fifty-five and pretty soon it was down to one by December 9, 2008.

Then, let us try to add the number of "work days left" (do not forget a Leap Year) until that January 9th date. Starting with January 1, 2008, there were "265 Work Days." It did not take long for that count down to be less than thirty work days. At each count down block, I would e-mail Kathy and family members just to keep it fresh, interesting, and fun. Of course, that count down clock with the "Actual Number of Days" kept our family informed when they visited.

Do some different things in the last year of full-time of employment. Try to break your normal routines and do things differently. Get out of the same routine. Take different routes to and from work. You will be surprised what has changed in your area over a short period of time. I know that gas is expensive, but try it.

What I found neat was how I dressed for work. I was brought up in those early years in the 1960's that office workers wore suits, ties, and dress shoes like my Dad taught me. Well, that has changed. Although that I am not completely in tune with the "dress down concept," I had changed my method of dress code to still be professional. For example, here is what I did the last year of employment:

1. One full week I would wear dress shirts and ties

2. The following week I would wear an open collar button down sport shirt

3. The next week (if in the winter) sweaters

4. Then rotate back to dress shirts and ties

5. Or, just mix it up!

This might seem strange to most of you. We at times are "clock watchers" just hoping that the days are going by faster. While wearing a watch, I found myself looking at it too much and the time went by very slowly. So, I stopped wearing a watch, especially to work. Notice when you go to a casino, there are no clocks around. It is a psychological method so that gamblers will not know the time of the day. This did make the days and weeks expedite toward January 9, 2009.

I always wore my hair full (not long) because of my natural curly hair. I hated it at times. It was hard to manage to appear neat in the days of suits and ties. Then my hair started to gray-- oh my. I knew that I was getting old. So, I had my hair cut into a spike look and used gel. WOW, that did make me feel a lot better. I thought it looked refreshing and lot of people said the same. However, there was one person who "loved my curly hair" and that is Kathy**. Sometimes you have to do things to make yourself feel better.

** Oh my, someone snuck a comment (footnote) in here:

"The Wife" is not a good or positive connotation! Editing by Pat..
"Love you……. Richard"

(The Daughter-in-Law)

Added Note: On 8-8-8, my son Greg and I got our hair cut. "A number-two razor" was used on the both of us. You guessed it. I got "butched" at the reluctance of the beautician. Washing out some of your gray hair can be tempting. Many people feel that gray hair is distinguished. I would love to do that. However, Kathy might not be too excited about it. Conclusion: Comprise

There Are Plenty of Ideas Floating Around. What Can You Add?

Yes, You Can Learn Something New

TEN

Enjoy Spending Your Money
But Stay Healthy At the Same Time

"What do you mean by that statement, Richard?" Meaning, Kathy and I worked together approaching the retirement years. We have invested and saved our financial resources. Now, it is our turn to enjoy our freedom. As not to be too redundant but to place the retirement subject in prospective, here are a few thoughts that come to mind during my preparation:

Travel Old Route 66

Work changing collection and credit report issues for seniors

Travel to warm weather parts of the country

Try camping and hiking

During the winter, take a walk at your local mall. A reminder, leave your credit cards at home

Join and swim at the local Senior Center or at the YMCA

Swim at your community pool

Volunteer at your community pool to work the main gate.

Be active in your Civic Association. Our Villa Belmont Condo Association (Newark, Delaware) is active. Most of the volunteer work is done by the senior citizens of the community. Volunteer to "police the area" picking up downed branches, keep your condo building flower beds fresh and weeded, help with the preparation to open the pool and then close it, and even run for a council seat on the Condo Association Board. I will assure you that it will not be dull.

Take a cruise or two

Now, the last one noted is taking a "cruise" (not *The Love Boat*). Going on a cruise can be very enjoyable and relaxing. However, it can be very stressful when it comes to the twenty-four hour eating opportunities. This is a big challenge that we all encounter. We also cannot rule out that temptation of the:

24 Hour of Happy Hours

How to overcome these temptations? I will be the first to admit that is not easy. What I have developed in my mind but have not totally implemented:

Make a self-pledge to control your mind when approaching the buffet table

Make a self-pledge to remember alcohol is not going to make you feel any better

Take in the cruise line library or computer room while at sea

Partake in the activities on a cruise ship while you are steaming from port to port

Walk from the bottom to the top deck. I mean take the steps

In the evening with your spouse, walk around the ship on the marked walk trails

On board, take in the dancing, stage shows and pool side activities

"Attitude Not Age Determines Energy"
(Robert Schuller)

How Would You Stay Fit While on Vacation?

_____

_____

_____

_____

_____

_____

_____

Please Learn The Components Of Life That Money Can Not Buy You

ELEVEN

Am I Too Old to Learn More?
Not Sure About This Chapter

On all the reading that we have done on retirement, it is stated to keep active with healthy activities and exercise. With old age setting in, our minds have a tendency to fade and our memories are not as sharp as they used to be. There have been articles written about going back to college just for the sake of going back to do something. I am in agreement to do something. Let me add a point here about college education. If you decide to take a college course, some colleges may not charge for senior citizens for the class they attend. I do not plan to return to school. However, I did enroll in American Sign Language 101.

You ask, again, why?

I had to accept the fact that I needed some assistance to hear Kathy and the grandchildren Fran, TJ, Elizabeth, Emily, Jessica, Nathan, and Kevin. My hearing is not getting much better as I age. Our oldest granddaughter Jessica successfully completed a semester of *American Sign Language* at Neumann College. Yes, I had to invest in hearing aids for each ear. However, I still have selected hearing.

Our youngest daughter Stephanie is currently a manager at American Eagle Outfitters in New Jersey. She and her friend Eric had worked with a young man who was deaf. They communicated with pen and paper. Our daughter-in-law Pat's parents John and Mildred are deaf. They are great people and are very patient with us.

Pat knows "signing" and our son Tim is learning it as well. We communicate with John and Mildred via note pad and pen until we learn "signing." I am now enrolled and taking *American Sign Language*. Is it easy? NO! However, it is a healthy a challenge.

What Educational Subject Would You Like to Learn?

____

____

____

____

____

____

Yes, You Will Continue To Learn and Become Educated In Something New

TWELVE

The Final Count Down

The Final Days
The Final Hours
The Final Minutes

You have prepared for this final day for years. The day has come. Just think back on how you felt graduating from high school, being honorably discharged from the service, starting and graduating from college, starting that new job, getting your business off the ground, getting married, or retiring. I wrote this only few weeks after my full retirement. I wanted to experience the full impact of retirement before putting it down on paper. I will warn you now that it is not as easy as you think it would be to retire. It will be a change in your mind how you have prepared mentally. Can you remember the following milestones in your life? Let me note mine:

I could not wait until I reached that teenage mile stone of thirteen years old

The next bracket was sixteen so I could drive

The next was eighteen years old

By that time, I graduated from high school

There was talk about changing the voting age

We could drink in New York State

At eighteen, I had to register for the draft

Oh, to be twenty-one. You know why!

The years just marched on after that

Then, fifty years old with a surprise party

Also at fifty, it is time to think about the future

Age sixty and another surprise party

Age sixty-five and a big family gathering

And, the day of retirement at sixty-five and a half

Those final weeks after you give your notice are the most exciting. You should continue with your daily work chores and communicate with your manager and/or supervisor on the transition. However, be prepared that you might not be asked to participate in the transition. Oh, you need to clean your work station; discard old and yellowed reports from the 1970's, 1980's, 1990's; update your policies and procedures; and keep trying to meet your personal goals and those set by management.

However, keep in mind, it is up to your manager and/or supervisor to keep you informed of what they want done during the transition leading to your last day. These are some thoughts that I clearly remember:

Final Month – You Are Becoming a "Civilian" Real Soon

I would suggest that you maintain your normal routine and composure. Be prepared for possible invitations to lunch or dinners. I had one offer and that was with my department manager.

Final Week – You Are Now A "Short Timer"

At the start of your last week of employment, management should have their game plan in line. You should be flexible to do some explaining of your duties. Have your policies updated and printed. If you are not asked, that is okay too. Just get ready to move on. You need just to prepare for the good times. My manager and supervisor appreciated those updated material.

Be prepared to meet with various levels of management and listen to their praises. However, if that does not come about, prepare further for your departure day. If they ask for suggestions, be positive and have a list prepared. If not asked, throw away your notes. If they did not care, you certainly do not have to care. If not done, start or finish cleaning up your work area. Keep in mind the retention dates of documents and forward any e-mails to management. E-mail attachments to your management group that they might find of interest. If they do not want it, they can discard it.

Final Day – All Down Hill from Here

This is your day, and you make it your day.

1. Management should have their game plan implemented. With the staff's support, our transition schedule was completed before my departure.

2. All work should be redistributed. All my duties were delegated to the other staff associates.

3. You should spend that last day tying up loose ends. The recipients of my duties were thoroughly trained.

4. Wish your coworkers "good luck."

5. Prepare those final e-mails to your coworkers, external contacts, friends, and family.

Final Hour
This Is Your "Hour of Power" (Robert Schuller)

You should be getting ready to be free as bird. You should be getting ready to do things your way. You need to be prepared for a final exit meeting with management. Let them invite you to that meeting. Again, if not asked, continue preparation for departure. My exit interview was conducted by my manager during the last day. He invited me out to lunch at a very nice restaurant. At that time, we discussed points of interest and matters that I thought could be improved with upper management support. That hour at lunch was a great gesture on his part, and I appreciated it.

Final Minutes – Oh My, It Is Almost Time to Leave

Let those farewell e-mails fly to whom you want. Turn in your items that are required. For example:

1. Identification badge

2. Parking tag parking pass

3. Reference books

4. Desk keys

Change your telephone out-going message. For example:

"Hi, this is Richard Beardsley. It is currently 3:30 p.m. (EST), Friday, January 9, 2009. This is my last day. Please do not leave a message. Contact one of the following:

Another alternative is programming your telephone to forward calls to a designed person selected by your manager and/ or supervisor.

Change your e-mail "Out of the Office Message"

"January 9, 2009, this is my last day of employment. Please contact the following:"

Now, It Is Time to Say Goodbye

Leave with a positive attitude and with nothing in your hands. If you have used a brief case as I did, leave it home the last two weeks. Let the vacation begin. Let the good times roll. Leave smiling and waving good bye. As I departed the building and went toward the parking lot, I turned to the American Flag that was flying gently in the January breeze and gave it a hardy Air Force salute. What a great feeling.

Now Let Us Celebrate

Meet your spouse at the usual place for a Friday afternoon rendezvous and celebrate the "Day of Reckoning." We had a family and friend happy hour gathering at my favorite restaurant (Matilda's Pub in Newark, Delaware). The restaurant staff and Kathy did a wonderful job in the preparation. The reception was fun for all. I was so happy that my parents were able to attend.

"Thanks for the Memories"
(Bob Hope)

55

_____

_____

_____

_____

_____

_____

_____

_____

_____

_____

_____

Please Assure That You Have Good Self-Esteem And Humility As You Move To A New Career of Retirement

THIRTEEN

Oh, I am Not Superstitious, But ....

Foot Note: Do you know that casino hotels do not have a thirteenth floor.

We are going to skip this chapter number and let you list a few ideas or concepts that I have missed. For example, list some of your past coworkers and managers of all levels who have had a positive influence in your life and occupational career. Also, list some of your major accomplishments over the years both at work and on the domestic front. Make your notes before they slip your mind.

_____

_____

_____

_____

_____

Richard A. Beardsley

_____

_____

_____

_____

_____

_____

_____

I Can Do Something For Myself And Enjoy It

58

FOURTEEN

Is This Vacation Or The First Day of Retirement?
What Should I Do First?

Retirement is a challenge for you to prove that you can do it. As I have described throughout this text, preparation and setting your mind to positive attitudes are the biggest challenges. What is it going to feel like on that first Saturday after retiring the day before? Just like any other weekend morning. Do things that you and your spouse normally do.

What about the Sunday? Like any other weekend that you and your spouse do. For example, attend Church, shop, read the paper, watch football games, or have a big family gathering.

Now, it is Monday which is the first full day of retirement. What can be done?

Should I call in sick?

I called my manager and supervisor early on the first Monday morning leaving a voice-message thanking them for the good times and challenging times during my employment. In the message, I told them in a joking manner that I am calling in sick for the week and forever.

If your spouse is still working, which in my case, get up as usual and help with the typical chores. Now, it is time to implement your retirement plan. Keep in mind to stay flexible and to stay active.

Stay Organized. I have mentioned to stay flexible. However, on the other hand, there needs to be some structure. I would suggest to get organized and maintain a "To Do List." It does not have to be as detailed as when you were working. It will help you manage your time and focus on the priorities at hand. This will make you feel good.

Walk. Take walks around your neighborhood or at the local park. Get started and build up each day's walk two minutes. Soon you will be doing sixty minutes with ease.

Swim. Join a Senior Center with a pool or the "Y."

CPR Class. Sign up at the local fire hall. Our oldest daughter Ann Marie is a registered paramedic. I know that she could find an opening for people.

Remember Your Parents. If your parents are still living, spend time with them. Get them to their doctor and dental appointments. It is important to keep in touch with them. Do not be in denial while they age. Be part of their lives. Make it comfortable for them. Kathy and I are the primary caregivers for my eighty-nine year old parents until they move into assisted living.

Gotta *Clean House*. I tidy one room of our condo each day. By the time the weekend rolls around, Kathy will have nothing to do except relax.

Do the Laundry. It is okay for a "man" to do it! In our condo campus, many men do the laundry. The best conversations take place while washing clothes.

What Clothes to Keep and Those to Give Away. I worked in an office atmosphere. That meant that I had dress shirts, ties, dress up trousers, dress sweaters, and all kind of button-down sport shirts. There is no use keeping them if "you ain't gonna wear them." With retirement, it was going to be jeans and sweat shorts or jean shorts and t-shirts. I kept some dress clothes and donated many to our local charitable agencies.

Oh, Our Families. Help your kids with your grandchildren.

Write A Book. Will I get this book done before I die?

Be the Main-Man Chef. Prepare meals so when your wife gets home she does not have to struggle with it. Just do the best you can.

Plan Meals. Now, since my wife continued to work for an additional year, I had to step it up a notch to prepare meals. Plan ahead your choices for at least three days. The planning will make it so much easier on your time schedule.

Get Your Grill Heated Up. Cook some of the meats for meals that later can be popped in the microwave.

You Want To Be A Professor. Volunteer to conduct classes at the local community center or Senior Center.

You Want To Be A Speaker. Be a guest speaker at church gatherings, at your local civic association, at the local Senior Center, or at community meetings. Be like a politician and publicize your book.

Promote Your Book. Speak at various community meetings. Maybe I can be booked on *The Today Show* and *Good Morning America*.

My Wife Has a Good Idea. Kathy wants to work as a part-time consultant at her ex-employer.

Jar Your Memory. It is okay to remember and reminisce about the old days. Spend time putting albums together. Look back to see what good times you had and how well you have developed as a person during your life time. I recently was digging through old newspapers of while I was in the U.S. Air Force from 1963 to 1967. That was a great history lesson for me. In fact, I prepared an album with the highlights of those newspapers. I hope that the family will be as enthused as I was.

To be satisfied is to be motivated. To be challenged is to be a mentor for people who surround you. Look back at your work career when you were younger and "at the top of your game." What talents and abilities did you have? Those same qualities are still with you now. You just have to take your creativity and pursue that concept. Your inherited abilities will make you a stronger senior citizen. You can still sort out the right avenue to pursue. Train your mind to be creative; train your mind to have fun. Take a moment to brainstorm your thoughts.

What Would Be Your Normal Routine	What Would Be Your Retirement Game Plan	How Can You Organize Your Retirement Life

"Find A Need And Fill It"
(Robert Schuller)

FIFTEEN

Let Us Slow Down and Enjoy!
"We Have Come to the Last Dance"

The objective of this book is to give you a conceptual idea for the preparations of retirement and for retirement itself. There are so many subjects that can be added. However, I promised to keep this short and sweet, as well as not to be too redundant. This book also has provided you a method to jot down your thoughts as you read.

Retirement Will Only Make It the Way You Make It

For almost all my career at my place of employment, I was tagged with the nick name of "Mr. B." I am not sure how that came about. Maybe Richard Beardsley was too long. "Mr. B" has a rhythm to it. I was an internal auditor, then a system analyst, then a credit manager, and back to an analyst. I worked with many people who showed respect to me over the years. It was explained to me recently that "Mr. B" was the respect given to me as a long-term employee and the positions that I held. Sorry, off on a tangent again. In summary, all I suggest are the following:

Stay healthy is a high priority

Take *American Sign Language*

Stay away from the alcohol in excess

Stay away from smoking

Talk to your physician about weaning off medicine

Walk and just walk more

Register for a Five-K walk for charity

Exercise by doing one hundred sit ups

Swim and swim

Lift weights (that is not for me) if your doctor permits

Write a book

Do not be a "book worm"

Learn to relax with a round of golf

Change something by working with your local government

My sister Sandy and brother-in-law Fred had business cards made showing that they are retired and are traveling. That is a cool idea. Give these cards to people that you meet on your trips. Our retirement business cards reads: "Route 66 or Bust."

For heavens sake stop worrying about retirement, about leaving the work, about leaving a salary behind, and about leaving some friends behind. All this worry is going to shorten your life. So, relax and enjoy. Life expediency is now into the late 70's if you concentrate on being healthy and active.

If you could look beyond today or if you could know beyond today, it would be a perfect situation. However, it does not work that way. That is why you must set your retirement to be active. If you do not plan, you will miss enjoyment all the time.

Plan that trip on Route 66

Why a "Route 66 Trip?" Well, that was the main route from the 1930's to the 1960's that was used to travel from Chicago to LA. With President Dwight Eisenhower's law introducing the Interstate System in 1954, it practically killed what used to be main routes throughout this country. When I was a teenager in the summer of 1961, my family Dad, Mom, and Sandy traveled that entire route from Chicago to LA. I vaguely remember all the high points of the trip, but as my wife and I studied the recent literature, I can picture some of the points of interest. Much of Route 66 is gone, like a lot of other main highways that have been gobbled up by the Interstate System. I do recall my father finding gas for 18.9-cents per gallon. As our son Greg would say, "That was a very long time ago." Those days of 20-cents per gallon for gas are gone.

"Route 66 or Bust"

If I publish this book before that trip, I will follow up with another book detailing the good old days on that Route 66 trip and what retirement is really all about: The true side of the picture. Take that Route 66 trip, or whatever trip you always wanted to take.

Spend time with your family.

Keep up on technology such as digital televisions, digital cameras, GPS systems, the economy, cell phones, and computers. I am not suggesting for you to buy these things, but just to keep your mind sharp and up-to-date on the modern world. Keep your mind and memory sharp.

It is not unusual for retirees to consider relocating although this is not on our agenda. If that is being considered, think about the following:

1. Consider the surrounding environment

2. Study the air quality

3. Research the local and state property taxes

4. Assure the activities in the area are what you want

5. Review your finances at a new location

6. Consider your comfort level by leaving your home roots

7. Think what would make you happy in a new area

8. Consider the effects of a new life at the new location

9. Be peace of mind once you make that decision

***Take Care of Your Smile, It Adds Face Value.
Do You Know That Smiling Is Worth A Million Dollars?***

How Would You Improve Retirement Life

_____

_____

_____

_____

_____

_____

Keep Smiling, There Is More To Come

SIXTEEN

PS: Keep Your Personal Matters and Agenda Up-To- Date

There are a few matters that we all must take into consideration as we move into our senior years. These suggestions will make the later years more comfortable for you, for your spouse, and for the entire family.

Keep your *Will* up-to-date. Review it carefully to assure that all your requests are the way you want it. It is okay to discuss the *Will* with members of the family. The objective is to make sure the decisions are in place before that trip to "The Lord." Maybe this will be the theme of one of my future books—preparing a *Will*. Another important element is to consult a lawyer when updating your *Will*.

Do not forget those **Federal, Local Taxes, and Property Taxes Returns.** Get free advice at the local library, community centers, or Senior Center.

Your **funeral arrangements** can be incorporated with your *Will*. If not, then write your funeral arrangements and visit a funeral home for advice. You might be asked to prepay. That decision is up to you. I elected not to pay up front. Let me add that my parents did prepay for their funeral. We have met with the funeral home director and all is in order for them.

Think about **assisted living** before you are too old and end up in a **nursing home.** Kathy and I made a decision while in our fifties that we wanted to downsize to a condo, and we did. With condo living, we have no lawns to mow, no leaves to rake, no need to take the trash out to the road, and less living quarters to maintain. However, on the other side of the coin, we need to shovel out our own cars. The good thing is that we do not have to shovel driveways. If you do this type of work, take your time, check your pulse, and help your elderly neighbors. After a recent snow storm, one of our neighbors started clearing snow with a dust pan. Guess who jumped in to assist?

Do not resist assisted living. Here are some brainstorming ideas that will help you recognize that it is time for the move:

1. Diagnosed with Alzheimer's Disease (also known as AD)

2. Diagnosed with dementia

3. Living alone

4. Difficulty walking

5. Equilibrium is unstable

6. Walking unknowingly into dangerous situations

7. Not able to concentrate

8. Difficulty getting dressed

9. Forget taking required medication

10. Not getting dressed for the day

11. Not eating properly

12. Generally forgetting things and names

13. Anxiety is uncontrollable

14. Fear of being alone

15. Not able to control personal finances and the basic checkbook

16. Not able to make routine monthly payments

17. Not able to maintain day-to-day control of investments.

18. There are many examples of bills not being paid which in turn result in the discontinuing of service

Visit several assisted living complexes with your family. Get on their mailing list to receive their monthly newsletter. Just keep up-to-date on the new methods of growing old comfortably. Discuss with your primary care physician the concept of assisted living. Here some guidelines that we have learned while working in the health industry for thirty-seven years:

Yes or No

Is the facility Medicare and Medicaid approved?_____

Can financial plans be developed for senior living?_____

Is the facility Federal and State approved?   _____

Are they insured and bonded?   _____

What is the security on the campus?   _____

Is the staff thoroughly screened?   _____

Is there a patient care manager?   _____

Are there registered nurses?   _____

Is the medical staff fulltime or part-time?   _____

Yes or No

Are there therapists on board? _____

How are medications monitored? _____

What are the procedures for emergency situations?_____

Is there a partnership with moving advisors? _____

Is there a chaplain on campus? _____

How about a medical social worker? _____

How many meals are available? _____

Is there skilled care nursing on the same campus?_____

How do you shop for groceries and gifts? _____

What recreational activities are available? _____

How is U.S. Postal mail delivered? _____

What is available for the laundry? _____

Is there telephone service in your room? _____

Can a computer be used? _____

What type of transportation is available? _____

What assistance is there for medical issues,

taxes, and legal matters? _____

Discuss the facilities with the Better Business Bureau._____

In summary, when looking at assisted living, consideration should be given to the type of facilities on campus. Again, I say, keeping in good physical condition is one key to healthy living. Inquire about an indoor pool, exercise room, and walkway around the campus. Even ask about a restaurant on site so you can meet with friends and relatives. Keeping our minds sharp is another key to a good life. Ask about a library, computer room, and the type of classes that are offered. In fact, maybe you can conduct a class or two. Assisted living is an excellent choice to prevent burdening your children as you age.

My brother-in-law's parents Ned and Patti Eckfeldt downsized to an independent living complex. That was the right move for them because on the same campus is a skilled nursing facility. As we age, health issues start taking over. My parents Herb and June recently downsized to condo living. They live in the same building as Kathy and me. They occupy a suite on the floor below us at the other end of the building. At first, they were reluctant to move. Now, they say it was the best decision they have ever made. The laundry room is just a few walking steps down the hallway to the left. The disposal room is a few walking steps down the hall to the right. The mail box is right around the corner. They do not have to climb stairs to do laundry nor to the disposal area.

Personal Note: Mom insists on doing some of our laundry. Why do we allow this? It keeps her active and feeling good that she is helping us.

If living in a house or an apartment or a condo or anyplace, prepare your surroundings to be safe. Here are some thoughts that I learned over the years:

Have telephone numbers programmed for easy dialing

Have an alert system that is worn around the neck. Push a button when help is needed

Consider renovating bathroom with an easy step-in-step-out shower and/or tub

Install good lighting to reduce the chances of tripping and falling

Have the kids change the furnace filter at least twice a year

Check the smoke detector twice a year

Stay in touch with the family and neighbors

Take your medicine "like a good boy or girl"

Important
Oh, Those Last Minute Notes

_____

_____

_____

_____

_____

_____

_____

_____

_____

Yes, Developing Spiritually and Mentally Is A Commitment To Keep

SEVENTEEN

PS II: Cost Saving Tips

Earlier in this book, I documented ways to save for your future. We also need to think about methods to reduce costs in this time of unpredictable gas prices, increasing food prices, souring prices for heating, and whatever else a recession deals our way. Let me brainstorm some concepts that I have learned during my occupational finance days:

Prescriptions. Talk to your physician about reducing your medications, converting to generic medication, or eliminating some medicine. I was able to save $30.00 each month. A little bit more about generic prescriptions:

From the September 2008 *University Of California, Berkeley Wellness News Letter* as published by John Swartzberg, MD, Chair for the Editorial Board, describes generic prescriptions as follows:

> **"Generic prescriptions are as good as brand-name drugs. About two-thirds of the prescriptions in the United States are generic. According to the FDA, generic prescriptions have to meet the same rigorous standards."**

Important Note: You need to discuss options with you doctor.

Reduce Price for Prescriptions. Check with other pharmacies. Look at the large discount chains. Some of these stores offer generic prescriptions for $5.00. This is not the co-pay. I am not being compensated for this. The one large discount store is Wal-Mart and Walgreen's.

"And, I approve this statement"

Flu Shots are offered at many times free at a community center, drug store, the local Senior Center, or at Church.

Financial Assistance. Take advantage of any local, state, and federal financial aid. Ask about financial programs at your local hospitals.

Local Property and School Taxes. File for reductions for local property taxes. It might save you a few dollars.

Who Does Taxes? Go to the local library or Senior Center to get your taxes done free.

Home Telephone (Also known as land phone). Consider discontinuing Call Waiting and Caller ID. We did and saved us $15.00 a month.

Telephone Services. Since telephone deregulation, there is more competition. Investigate other telephone companies that you see advertised.

Long Distance. Find a cheaper long distance company. Again, I am not being compensated for this referral. We have Uni-Tel as our long distance carrier.

Cell Phone Versa Home Phone. Think about discontinuing your home land telephone and use only your cell phone as the primary method of verbal communication.

Save Gas. For us "baby boomers," we can remember when gas was 20-cents a gallon plus receiving *Green Stamps.* Not now-a-days. This is one of the biggest issues facing Americans. Do not stop driving, but drive smarter. We have to combine trips, drive when there are no traffic delays, consider public transportation, or even car pool.

Paying Bills without Postage. With postage stamps increasing more frequently, there are other methods to pay bills. Buy *U.S. Forever Postage Stamps.*

1. **Banks.** Some banks accept payments for certain utilities. When going to the bank for personal business, pay other bills at the bank and stop at other locations.

2. **When on the road** for other business, plan to stop at the store to pay your bill personally. I must emphasize do not make a special trip just to pay a bill. Combine it with other trips.

3. **Internet.** Pay through the web. I must admit that I am not too excited about using this method, but I will have to learn to be confident that it is secure.

4. **Debit Card.** Pay bills via telephone with a debit card. However, you cannot pay a bank credit card with another credit card. This will save the use of checks and, therefore, you will not have to reorder checks as frequently. I need to be more confident about doing this. And, I will do it!

Cable or Dish. If you have cable or a dish, are there other packages that can reduce you monthly fee? In other words, do you really need all those channels? This is just another thought on my part.

Home Renovations. Plan what projects that you and your spouse want to do with your home or condo. For example, we planned two or three years out to replace our kitchen and bathroom floors, replace a couple appliances, install new window covering, and install a couple light-fans. All the projects were completed and paid off before Kathy and I were fully retired.

Computer. Look into Internet service for home or go to the library. Stay in touch with your family. It could be cheaper than calling long distance.

Newspapers. Do you really need to receive the daily and Sunday newspapers? Another thought on my part. With the Internet, with twenty-four hours of television and radio news, why read it, when you can see it and/or hear it.

Magazines. Do you really need the magazines you receive? You can catch up on your light reading at your local library, at the local Senior Center, and at your doctor and dentist appointments. That is money saved right there.

Car or Cars. Review your vehicle situation:

1. Do you need two cars?

2. Can you have a larger deductible?

3. Drop some of incidental automobile insurance coverage such as towing and road side service (use your cell phone).

4. Consult your agent before making any decisions.

NOTE: Our Progressive Insurance Agent, who also is an independent agent, suggested a transfer of our policy to another insurance company. We are considered "good drivers" which means no accidents or traffic tickets. That change is saving us about $75 annually. Every little bit saved goes to happier times.

Credit Cards. Get all your credit card bills paid off before you retire. Subsequently, discard some or all the credit-debit cards. I did. I now retain two cards and feel great being able to do that.

Car Loan. Pay off your car loan.

Mortgage. Pay off your mortgage. Did you know that you can pay off your mortgage early by making extra payments on the mortgage principle? The lending companies do not want you to know this.

Buy What? Then, only buy if you really need it and not charge it. That is why I say when you go to The Mall to walk, leave your credit cards at home.

Financial Institution Award Point. On the other hand, some banks and credit institutions offer "Award Points" for charging purchases. Please plan to pay the bill off on the first cycle to prevent interest charges.

Oh, Those Tough Family Decisions. Your family will have to understand that gifts for birthdays, Christmas, anniversaries, and other special occasions will not be as lavish. Give gift cards or just money. We did discuss this subject with our families in detail, so they understood what the future would bring.

"Hat Trick" (This is not the Hockey Hat Trick). Consider "Family Christmas Drawings." Instead of buying gifts for each adult, you would buy for only the one you drew from the hat. In our family, it is called "Secret Santa."

Those Special Days. Do your shopping on Senior Days. You can save ten to twenty percent.

Do Not Shop Harder But Shop Smarter. When grocery shopping, use the coupons found in the newspaper, magazines, or printed off the Internet. You will be surprised what you save.

Lunch and Dinner. Also, look for coupons that save from $3.00 to $10.00 on a lunch and/or dinner.

Eating In. Plan to eat your meals in rather than out every day. That will save gas, save money, and save your weight from going up like gas prices.

Eat Early. Take advantage of the "early bird" specials. If nobody recognizes you are a senior citizen, ask if they have a senior discount. *Denny's* started senior discounts at age fifty-five.

More Paper Work. Ask your kids to scan the newspapers for coupons.

That Loose Change. We have a bank at home (like our kids did and still have) and throw loose change and paper money saved on coupons. It is amazing how that builds up over a period of several years. In fact, our *Bud Light Bank* is going toward our Route 66 trip. Maybe I will count it before publishing this book.

At Night Too Late for Entertainment. Take in the movies during the day when the admission price is cheaper.

Take Advantage of the Kids. If you have downsized as we did, you might not have a washer and dryer in your suite. However, you probably have coin operated machines. In our condo building, we have the coin operated machine. You can take advantage of the kids. While sitting for the grandchildren in their home, you use the child care time as your laundry time. This will save you $15.00 to $20.00 a week.

Oh, To Be a Teenager Again. Take a driver's education class. It could save you up to an additional 10% on your auto insurance.

Join a Club or Two. It might be worthwhile to join AAA and ARRP. These clubs have senior discounts as well as cost saving ideas.

Get Rewarded. If you use a credit or debit card, investigate the "Reward Points" program. It will save you money to use for gift cards and even airline tickets.

Other Ideas. Another publication is *The AARP Bulletin.* Again, there articles geared toward seniors. The subjects range from A to Z. I have discovered that these publications are very helpful to Kathy and me.

Men Hair Cuts. Now, this might sound weird. Consider having your wife or a member of your family cut your hair. **Breaking News:** I have just learned that there are "gal barbers" in our family. To get my hair done costs $17.00 (including tip). That is more money to dump in your coin bank.

Planning a Trip? It will be to your advantage to book your trip via the Website rather than a travel agent. We have learned that this method to be very successful.

What about Driving. I might as well put this point here. As the aging process continues, we need to seriously consider how much longer we can continue to drive. I have known of many cases that the elderly have given up driving and transferred the car to a relative. I know that is a difficult decision. However, there is savings right there.

It Is Time for you to Brainstorm Your Cost Cutting Ideas

_____

_____

_____

_____

_____

_____

"A Penny Saved Is A Penny Earned""
(Benjamin Franklin)

EIGHTEEN

I Think That I Am Losing Count

With technology expanding each day by leap and bounds, the computer is almost a way of life. Even at our ages, the use of a computer is beneficial as a learning tool. Below are a few suggested Internet web sites that Kathy has researched. I hope that it will help you as well.

www.aarp.com

www.socialsecurity.gov

www.medicare.gov

www.Erickson.com

www.EricksonTribune.com

www.aaa.com

www.resolutionizeretirement.com

www.transitionnetwork.org

www.hotels.com

www.travelocity.com

Richard A. Beardsley

www.habitat.org

List Your Web Sites

_____

_____

_____

_____

_____

Do Not Feel Lost With A Computer, It Will Work For You

NINETEEN

Let Us Wrap It Up

The objective of this book is to give you a bird's eye view of the preparation for retirement. I can only add a few final thoughts. Think positive as you move toward retirement. Once you make the final decision, go for it and enjoy it. When you finally step out of your company doors for good, be sure to look at the future in a positive light because your new life is about to begin. There is no need to look back. When I departed my place of employment on that last day of January 9, 2009, it was a quiet departure. That is the way that I wanted it. It was a great week with an office dinner at the local Hilton Restaurant. Later in the week my manager and supervisor had another organized farewell. Other long-known coworkers arrived as a great surprise. It was a great farewell.

I will comment diplomatically. Top management did not attend the farewell dinner or the farewell tea. However, I must also note that I never received a note from upper management. That is okay. My manager and supervisor did attend both engagements. I appreciated those farewell gatherings very much. Middle management elected not to attend the farewell dinner but did attend the farewell tea at the end of the week. Top management elected not to attend either. No e-mail or telephone was received from them.

My manager did invite me to lunch on my last day. That also was my exit interview. I highly appreciated that opportunity to discuss my concepts to improve my position. At the end of day on January 9, 2009, I presented my supervisor with my desk keys, with my parking pass, and with my identification badge.

It is not difficult for me to add a closing thought or two. I have put together a concise concept for the preparation for retirement. This book is addressed to adults approaching or seriously looking to the future of retirement. This book also is text book for young adults for the early preparation of retirement. It is up to you as what you want to do.

Recently, I was sorting papers from old boxes. I found a number of newspapers from the United States Air Force for 1964 and 1966. I want to quote part of an article directly from *The Citrus Flyer* published by McCoy Air Force Base in Orlando, Florida. The date of the article is April 24, 1964. The author was Colonel Stanley L. Hand, Commander 306th Bombardment Wing. The newspaper is yellowed and nearly shredded. Colonel Hand's words in 1964 fit today:

> "There is an old saying that a river becomes crooked by following the lines of least resistance. So do men (and women)! Life is growth. Controlled growth is personal development; wild growth is personal waste. The man (woman) who lives by whim and fancy, by pulse and emotion, who gives into every temptation, has thrown away his power of will. Only by retracing our past carelessness, we can break bad habits and develop good habits for the future. Let's take the first step of that journey today!"

Now, it is time to finalize this "masterpiece" and for you to draw your conclusions on your own game plan. This world has changed over the years to the point that we must live each day at a time. Since "9-11", our lives have changed that make it more challenging and inconvenient to travel. With the terrorist activity throughout the world, no one is safe. However, we must find unity and inter-strength to keep going. With these inconveniences, you must travel at your leisure and accept the hassles of security. It is for your safety.

Like what I tell all our kids and more recently our grandchildren:

Be Alert....Be Careful....Be Safe....And Enjoy

Thank you

And

Good Bye

Think How You Can Turn A Negative Situation Into A Positive Event

Appendix

How About Some Sample Letters

I am one who believes that when you sneeze, you should document it. As part of my military training, college education, and occupational training, I believe in recording my thoughts for further consideration. As I mentioned earlier in this text, discussions on retirement plans need to be specific and very clearly presented. To assure that the staff and family totally understand, here are a few sample letters.

E-mail to Management to Schedule a Meeting

DATE: October 3, 2008

I want to schedule a meeting with you Tuesday, October 7, at 9:00 a.m. in your office. I am told by your secretary that you have some open time. This is a very important meeting as we need to discuss my future ambitions with Christiana Care Health Services.

Thank you.....................Richard

Sample Letter to Present Your Managers at the Start of the Meeting

DATE: October 7, 2008

Kathy and I have decided that it is a good time for me to retire. My last day of work will be Friday, January 9, 2009, departing the area at 1530 hours.

I have to admit that this is one of the easiest decisions that I have had to make in a life time. I have done all that I can for this company. It is time for my wife, my family, and me to enjoy the better things in life before we get too old to enjoy them.

Kathy and I have worked a number of years up to this date of decision. We have consolidated all the information together to assure that this is the right time. And, it is the perfect time with my age and for our comfortable financial security. With this announcement, it gives the Finance Department of Christiana Care Health Services an opportunity to reorganize our area.

Thank you for the good times and for the challenging times..................Richard

Confirmation E-Mail to Management

DATE: October 7, 2008

First, I want to thank you for taking time to discuss my retirement plans. It was a decision that all people have to make at some point in their life. This confirms our discussions this morning. I will officially be retiring on Friday, January 9, 2009.

(Here is a good place to insert a statement that you are willing to assist in the transition and to list those transition points).

It has been a great pleasure to work for this organization for thirty-seven plus years. There have been peaks and valleys with this company over the years. However, this is now one of the best hospitals in the United States. I am proud to have been part of that development.

Thank you................Richard

E-mail To Your Co-Workers Announcing Your Retirement

DATE: October 7, 2008

Good morning, All.....................

I want to let my coworkers know that I have met with management. I have given them notice that I plan to retire. My last day will be on Friday, January 9, 2009.

Yes, I am at the ripe old age of sixty-five and half. You might ask why am I leaving now and not at an earlier age. Well, my wife is a few years younger than me. If I retired earlier, I would have to stay home and take care of the laundry, dishes, fix my lovely wife lunch as she leaves for work, and have dinner on the table when she arrives home.

So, you can see my reasoning to stay. Also, I know that this company needed me.   Hee.............Hee!

We have a few weeks for our management group to decide what is going to happen with this position. During that time, we all need to continue to work together and meet our personal goals as well as those set by our management group.

It has been a wonderful thirty-seven plus years. Now, it is time for Kathy and me to move on. Let us enjoy the next few weeks as we approach to January 9, 2009.

Thank you.................Richard

The Final Farewell E-mail to Your Co-workers

DATE: January 9, 2009

To My Fellow Work Friends:

Well, it is time to say that *We Have Come To The Last Dance.* In a few minutes, it will be the "The Retired Life of Mr. B." It will be a new beginning for a gentleman who is eager to grow old slowly and not have to use my Medicare Card too often.

We have had a great couple months since giving my notice for the opportunity to enjoy retirement. All I can say is thank you for all the good times. YES, there were a few challenging times, too. However, those challenges in life, whether at work or at home, are good for our life style to make us appreciate life.

Thank you all for the great time. You will be fine.

Gone, but not forgotten but to shovel snow. Let the party begin.

Mr. B

Let Those Final E-Mails Fly Because "You Have Come to the Last Dance"

Now Start Enjoying Your Retirement

About the Author

Richard A. Beardsley was born in Niagara Falls, New York, to Herbert and June Beardsley in 1943.

Richard is a sixty-six year old down home type guy. He graduated from Mount Pleasant High School in Wilmington, Delaware, in June of 1962. He attended Rochester Institute of Technology in Rochester, New York. However, he realized that his talents were needed in the United States Air Force. Richard served four years of which one was in Vietnam during 1966. During his last three months of service in Vietnam, he applied to several colleges. Back in those days there was no e-mail nor fax access from any place in world as there is now. At that time, there was no capability of placing calls back to the United States of America. Before his honorable discharge from the United States Air Force in 1966, Richard was accepted at Goldey Beacom College in Wilmington, Delaware, where he majored in Accounting and Business Administration. After he earned Associates Degree, Richard attended Hiram Scott College in Scottsbluff, Nebraska. There he earned his Bachelors Degree in Accounting and Business Administration.

Richard worked in his hometown of Wilmington-Newark, Delaware, for over forty years – spending over thirty-seven years with the Christiana Care Health Systems. After a long work career in the United States health industry, Richard has an excellent concept of retirement and the preparations for retiring especially with the health care system and retirement preparation in America. Richard knows the "ins and outs" of the retirement and is adverse in the field of preparing for retirement and how it correlated with health care and the extensive range of preparation for retirement.

What led Richard to write this book was self-motivation to alert the general public on the concept of preparing for retirement in America. Richard's back ground is very precise and accurate after preparing for the good days in life. While employed at Christiana Care Health Services in Newark, Delaware, for over thirty seven years, Richard was an Internal Auditor. Four years later was promoted to Systems Auditor for Computer Operations. Subsequently, three years later promoted Credit Manager, and an Assistant Director of the Business Office.

What qualifies Richard to write this book? His knowledge of the health industry and the process was able to document detailed policy and procedures at his place of employment. These policies involved detailed procedures on job functions, on privacy guidelines, on methods to process charge collection, on the collection of patient information, on obtaining and verifying health insurance, on collecting payments for elective procedures, and on determining eligible for admission to the hospital.

Richard and his wife Kathy share five children and seven grandchildren. All of their siblings are successful in their careers.